This book belongs to:

_____

To read with:

_____

PICTURE SQUIRRELS

First published in 2017 in Great Britain by Barrington Stoke Ltd
18 Walker Street, Edinburgh, EH3 7LP

www.picturesquirrels.co.uk

Text © 2017 Vivian French
Illustrations © 2017 Nigel Baines

The moral right of Vivian French and Nigel Baines to be identified
as the author and illustrator of this work has been asserted in
accordance with the Copyright, Designs and Patents Act, 1988

A CIP catalogue record for this book is available from the British
Library upon request

ISBN 978-1-78112-602-8

Printed in China by Leo

For the wonderful staff and children of
Our Lady and St Anne's RC Primary School,
Newcastle – V.F.

For all children who feel like they
are a little different – N.B.

VIVIAN FRENCH

NIGEL BAINES

THE COVERS OF MY BOOK ARE TOO FAR APART!

(and other grumbles)

PICTURE SQUIRRELS

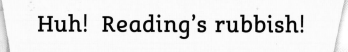

Come and see me in the library. Tell me what you like and I'll find something for you to try.
You don't have to read books. Comics are cool too.
I like to find out how to do stuff.
I like joke books. What do you get if you cross a sheepdog with a jelly?
The collie-wobbles!

I read in bed before I go to sleep.

My stepdad reads in the bath. He's in there for HOURS!

I read when I'm meant to be tidying my room. Don't tell my mum!

I read when I have boring stuff to do, like shopping with my sister.

I read while the dinner's cooking. Sometimes I burn things!

You don't have to read books. Comics are cool too. Hang on! I've said that before ... But it's still true.
Do you have a favourite film or show? Try reading a book about it.
Or a favourite sport or hobby? I like ballet dancing – and football!

I do think the cover of this book will put boys off. That's a shame.
I read all my sister's books, and she reads all of mine.
I always read a couple of pages before I decide if a book's for me or not.

My dad and I both love stories. We snuggle up to read them together.
Sometimes Mum reads to me, and sometimes I read to her!
Even my dog likes to join in!

The End ...

Nearly but not quite.

Now you've read this book,
how about you ...

Grow a love of reading

PICTURE SQUIRRELS